THE HAUNTING OF DUNGEO[...] K

Phil Roxbee Cox

Illustrated by
Jane Gedye

Series Editor: Gaby Waters
Assistant Editor: Michelle Bates

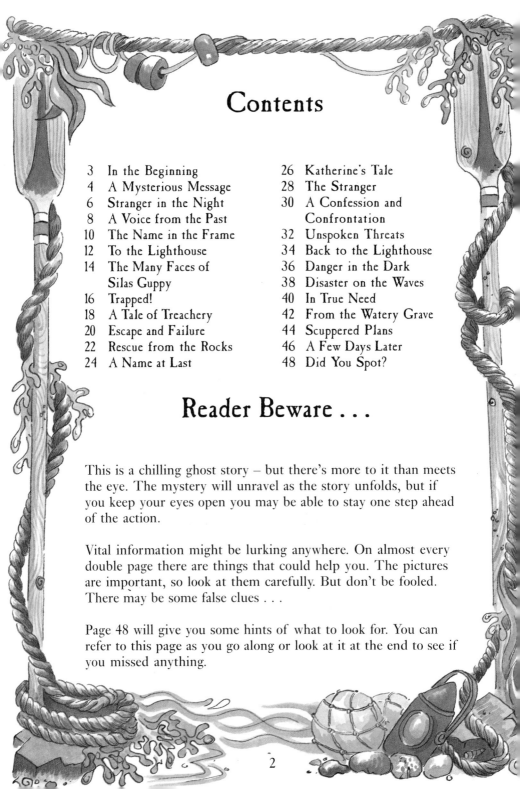

Contents

3 In the Beginning
4 A Mysterious Message
6 Stranger in the Night
8 A Voice from the Past
10 The Name in the Frame
12 To the Lighthouse
14 The Many Faces of
Silas Guppy
16 Trapped!
18 A Tale of Treachery
20 Escape and Failure
22 Rescue from the Rocks
24 A Name at Last

26 Katherine's Tale
28 The Stranger
30 A Confession and
Confrontation
32 Unspoken Threats
34 Back to the Lighthouse
36 Danger in the Dark
38 Disaster on the Waves
40 In True Need
42 From the Watery Grave
44 Scuppered Plans
46 A Few Days Later
48 Did You Spot?

Reader Beware . . .

This is a chilling ghost story – but there's more to it than meets the eye. The mystery will unravel as the story unfolds, but if you keep your eyes open you may be able to stay one step ahead of the action.

Vital information might be lurking anywhere. On almost every double page there are things that could help you. The pictures are important, so look at them carefully. But don't be fooled. There may be some false clues . . .

Page 48 will give you some hints of what to look for. You can refer to this page as you go along or look at it at the end to see if you missed anything.

In the Beginning

What later became a strange and terrifying adventure for brothers Boz and JJ started simply enough with a stroll around a local market. The weather was sunny, and the place was the fishing village of Dungeon Creek.

"Wow!" said Boz, picking up an old pistol. "This would be a great present to buy Mr. Barkis as a thank you for letting us stay with him. Then he saw how much it cost. "Err, perhaps not," he added, hurriedly putting it down.

They spent another hour at the market, which sold everything from fish to furniture. This was much more fun than shopping at home. If JJ hadn't tripped and landed flat on his face, they might have avoided all the trouble that lay ahead – unless, of course, other strange forces were at work that day. But JJ did trip and, as he picked himself up and put his glasses back on, something caught his eye. A glint of gold winked at him from under a blanket.

JJ pulled back the blanket. The gold was an ornately carved wooden picture frame. Boz stepped back to study his brother's find. It was an oil painting, dark with age. "We must buy this painting, JJ," he said strangely. "We must own it. The painting has to be ours."

3

A Mysterious Message

Boz and JJ took the painting straight back to the cottage where they were staying with their parents' friend, Mr. Barkis. This place was so old that the timbers were all crooked and the floors weren't even level. There weren't any cottages like that back in their home town.

"Look what we've just bought," said JJ, plonking the painting down in front of Mr. Barkis, who was reading a spooky book about a ghost train.

Their host picked up the picture. "You bought this at the market?" he asked, studying their purchase carefully. "It must be at least two hundred years old, you know. How much did it cost you?" When they told him, he was impressed. "It must be worth more than that," he said. JJ and Boz knew that Mr. Barkis must have some idea what he was talking about. He made his living making and selling copies of antique furniture.

Mr. Barkis put down the painting and left the room. He went out to his workshop and crashed around for a while. He returned with a triumphant look on his face and a bottle and a cloth in his hands.

What's that for, Mr. Barkis?

You'll see.

4

He poured some liquid from the bottle onto the cloth, then gently began to rub the painting with it. The result was dramatic. Centuries of grime were wiped away in an instant. What had been dull areas of brown now revealed their original glow. Bold brushstrokes were shown off in all their glory.

"I thought the dark shape at the front was supposed to be a rock," Boz pointed. "But it's a woman . . . and the sea really looks as if it's moving. In fact, it makes me feel queasy just looking at it."

SI RE VERA ME REQUIRIS DIC NOMEN MEUM TUM TIBI ADSTABO

"And what have we here?" said Mr. Barkis, with a final rub of the cloth. "It's writing." He leaned forward and peered at it, his nose almost touching the canvas. "Hmm. How very strange. How very interesting."

"They don't look like any words I've ever seen before," said JJ, trying to see past Mr. Barkis's head. His glasses were steaming up in the heat of the room.

"That's because they're written in Latin," said Barkis.

"What do they mean?" asked Boz. He ran his fingertips across the painted letters. They felt icy cold. He shuddered. His mind was filled with a strange sense of urgency. "We have to find out what they mean . . . "

5

Stranger in the Night

That night, only their third in Dungeon Creek, JJ and Boz were awoken by a loud CRASH from downstairs. "What was that?" said JJ sitting bolt upright. He banged his head on the bottom of Boz's bunk above him.

"It sounded like breaking glass," said Boz, sitting up with a start. He banged his head on the ceiling. "Ouch! Perhaps Mr. Barkis just stretched and put his elbow through the window," he grinned. "This cottage isn't very big."

"It's three o'clock in the morning. Even *he* must be in bed by now," said JJ, lowering his voice to a whisper. "Let's go downstairs and investigate. It could just be a cat."

Cautiously, they crept out of their bedroom, across the sloping landing to the bannisters. They then edged their way down the rickety old stairs – step by creaking step – sometimes stopping for fear of being heard. Their hearts began to beat faster as they tiptoed into the moonlit room. This was no cat. The boys had walked in on a burglary. In the moonlight streaming through a broken window, they could make out the shadowy form of *someone about to make off with their painting!*

Boz wished that he was carrying the old pistol they'd seen at the market. JJ wished that he was three feet taller and didn't wear glasses. Neither of them was sure of the best way to tackle a real live burglar caught in the act, but they had to do something.

JJ mouthed the words "What shall we do?" without making a sound, but his brother understood him.

"Stay right where you are!" Boz called out, in the deepest voice he could muster. The intruder did the exact opposite, dropping the painting and scrambling out of the window. The brothers rushed over to the window. They glimpsed the outline retreating before it disappeared into the night. Both were sure that they had seen the silhouetted figure somewhere before.

A few moments later, the front door flew open and a light went on. Barkis stepped into the room carrying a pile of firewood. "What on earth are you two doing up at this time of night?" he asked with a puzzled frown.

"We've just chased off a burglar who was trying to steal our painting," explained JJ. "He got away through the window."

"Really?" said Mr. Barkis. "The thieving swine must have waited for me to slip out to my workshop before sneaking in. Good work, boys." He didn't sound particularly concerned. Boz suggested they call the police. Mr. Barkis dropped a log on his own foot. "That won't be necessary," he said quickly. "The only harm done is a broken window, and that's easily fixed in the morning. Back to bed the pair of you." So back to bed they went. But Boz and JJ didn't sleep a wink.

A Voice from the Past

When Boz and JJ went downstairs the next morning, Mr. Barkis had already made their breakfast and was busy mending the broken window. Boz's eyes fixed on the painting. The image of the woman staring out of the canvas had filled his thoughts throughout his sleepless night. It was almost as if she had been trying to call out to him.

"Interested in the Latin inscription on your painting?" asked Mr. Barkis, interrupting his thoughts. Boz nodded, his mouth full of toast. "Then you should go and see Mr. Tigg at the schoolhouse. Latin used to be taught in most schools a long time ago, and Mr. Tigg became a teacher a very long time ago indeed." He closed the window, chuckling to himself.

"Let's copy down the inscription rather than lug a valuable two-hundred-year-old oil painting around Dungeon Creek with us," JJ suggested. Boz had to admit it was a good idea.

"I don't want to dampen your excitement," said Mr. Barkis. "But I didn't say your picture was *valuable*. I simply said that it's worth more than you paid for it. I wouldn't start planning any exotic trips abroad just yet if I were you." He closed the window and put the lid on his tin of putty.

"Somebody thought it was worth stealing," JJ reminded him. "I'm not sure what else they would want from here." Mr. Barkis glared at the boy. "Er, no disrespect, Mr. Barkis," JJ added hurriedly.

JJ and Boz found Mr. Tigg at the schoolhouse. He was outside raking up leaves. JJ explained who they were, and asked if he would mind translating some Latin for them.

Without a word, the old man dropped his rake and marched into the schoolhouse. Boz and JJ were beginning to wonder whether they'd said something to upset him, when he returned wearing a pair of glasses.

"Can't read a thing without them," he said. JJ handed him the piece of paper with the words copied onto it. "Hmm. It's straightforward enough," said the old teacher.

SI RE VERA ME REQUIRIS DIC NOMEN MEUM TUM TIBI ADSTABO

"We thought *vera* might be a woman's name," said Boz. "And *tibi* a cat's, but we were stuck after that."

"No, no, no," groaned Mr Tigg. "What your mysterious inscription says is, '*if you truly need me, say my name and I shall be there to aid you*'."

Boz repeated the words. "*If you truly need me, say my name and I shall be there to aid you*. What a strange message. I wonder who it was meant for? '*Say my name*' must mean the name of the woman. She's the only person in the painting." He had to find out her name. He just *had* to. Meanwhile, a pair of unblinking eyes watched the three of them from nearby.

The Name in the Frame

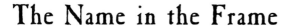

Back at the cottage, Mr. Barkis peered at the canvas through a special kind of magnifying glass. He held it up to his eye and bent over the painting. Boz was convinced that the woman's name must be written somewhere on the canvas. Mr. Barkis handed the eyeglass to Boz.

"Her name must be hidden somewhere in the picture," said Boz. "It probably won't be too obvious. After all, it's tied up with that cryptic Latin message. Finding her name should help us make sense of what it all means."

JJ agreed. "I expect whoever painted this didn't want her name to be too easy to find," said JJ. "After all, the message telling us to find her name was written in Latin to make it difficult to understand."

Barkis sat down in his chair and picked up his book about the ghost train. "When that message was written, plenty of people would have understood Latin," he pointed out. "And isn't it '*say* my name' not '*find* my name'?"

Boz said nothing, then his brother whooped with delight. "Look," said JJ. "I've found a name . . . but it doesn't sound like a woman's." He pointed.

"That must be the name of the painter," Boz sighed. His face fell.

"It's a good start though," said Mr. Barkis. "The name Guppy sounds familiar. Why not go down to the library and look it up there?"

Boz and JJ put their jackets back on and left the cottage for the second time that day. As they walked down the overgrown path to the gate, they saw Mr. Barkis disappear into his workshop.

"I like Mr. Barkis," said JJ. "But there is something a little mysterious about him. Don't you think so?"

His elder brother shrugged. "It's the painting I find mysterious," he said. The image of the woman on the rocks flashed through his mind.

The two boys began walking down the country lane which led to the village. At that moment, there was the ring of a bell, and an elderly woman on an even older bicycle whizzed past them at great speed.

"That was the lady who sold us the painting!" cried Boz. "Perhaps she can tell us more about it."

They called after the woman but either she didn't hear them, or she chose to ignore their calls. Boz and JJ chased after her but, moments later, she had disappeared around a bend.

"Perhaps she thinks we're a pair of dissatisfied customers who want our money back," JJ grinned. Bending forward to catch his breath, he rested his arm on a gate at the side of the road. His brother's eyes widened in amazement. "What is it?" JJ demanded.

Boz pointed to two small words on a letter box.

SILAS GUPPY

To the Lighthouse

Intrigued, Boz and JJ pushed open the gate and began to follow a very long and winding path. It led them through coarse grass, past thorny bushes, in the direction of the sea.

"This is weird," said JJ. "It's like a case of *déjà vu*."

"Isn't that the place in France where crazy Cousin Colin lives?" asked Boz. JJ groaned. He couldn't tell whether his brother was joking or not.

"It's a feeling that you've been somewhere before, even though it's really the first time you've been there," JJ explained. "I feel that now."

"That's exactly how I'm feeling too," said Boz excitedly. Their surroundings were strangely familiar. It was almost as if they were experiencing someone else's memory of the place. For the umpteenth time, the image of the woman in the painting flashed through Boz's mind.

Suddenly, the sun disappeared behind a cloud, and the gloomy light made the sea seem strangely different. The waves looked like the vivid brushstrokes of oil paint. No wonder. This was the very stretch of coastline in the picture!

The path took them down to the shore, and ended right in front of a stretch of rocks leading all the way out to an offshore lighthouse. The lighthouse rose majestically into the cloud-filled sky

All feelings of uneasiness were forgotten in an instant. "This is fantastic," said JJ. Together they set off across the rocks, the seawater lapping at their ankles.

The boys reached the lighthouse to find the door slightly open. "I never thought I'd get to go inside a real lighthouse," said Boz. "Come on!"

"Shouldn't we knock, or something?" suggested JJ, a little nervously. "If the door's open it probably means that someone's at home."

"If they are, they'll never hear us down here," replied Boz. "We'll shout out on the way up."

The boys went inside and began climbing the cold dark stairs. The place smelled musty with age and dank with salt water. JJ began to feel breathless, and it wasn't just the climb. The air was getting more and more stale with every step.

They paused to catch their breath. Then, just as they were about to set off again, they heard a strange flapping noise up ahead in the echoing gloom. Nervously, Boz stepped forward. Beating wings flapped around him, fanning air against his cheek. He cried out in terror.

13

The Many Faces of Silas Guppy

Boz and JJ laughed with relief when they realized what the creature was. This was no huge and terrifying bat but only a cheeky myna bird.

"Hullo boys! Hullo boys!" cried the bird, circling above their heads as they made their way up to an open door. The brothers wondered if there were any other occupants inside the lighthouse.

Boz knocked. "Is there anybody there?" he called out, just in case a lighthouse keeper was lurking in the shadows. They still felt a bit shaken by the bat that wasn't a bat. The silence was broken by another squawk from the bird. Boz pushed the door open wide.

They found themselves in a large round room. What struck JJ and Boz was the furniture. It must have been specially made for the lighthouse. The lighthouse walls were curved, and so was the back of the furniture. It all fitted perfectly, but would look very out of place in an ordinary house.

Boz's eyes were drawn to the pictures hanging on the far side of the room. Some were drawings, some were paintings, and some were photographs. Each was a picture of a man and under each and every one of them was a different date, but the same name. The name was Silas Guppy. In an instant, Boz was reminded of what had first led them down the path and to this place. He had forgotten in all the excitement.

JJ came over and stood by his brother. He gasped. They studied the pictures together in silence. Surely they were all of the same man? Okay, so his hair was different in each picture, but his features were the same. "This is crazy" JJ protested. "The earliest picture is dated two hundred years ago, but some of them are only a few years old!"

"And, if Guppy painted our picture of the woman with the mysterious Latin message on it, what's he doing smiling at us out of a photo dated nineteen ninety?" Boz gulped. "I'm beginning to think there's something weird about Dungeon Creek and not just the painting." At that moment, the curved door behind them slammed shut, as if pulled by some invisible hand. It left the brothers with a loud THUD ringing in their ears.

Trapped!

The door wouldn't budge. JJ and Boz pushed it and pulled it. JJ even punched it, but that was more in frustration than thinking it would do any good. The door stayed firmly shut.

"Perhaps there's another way out of here," Boz suggested.

"I don't see how," sighed JJ. "The stairs ended on the other side of the door, and that ladder over there must lead up to where the light is."

> Do you think it was the wind?

> Sure. What else could have slammed it shut?

"Then we'll have to try to lever the door open. Let's see if we can find something to slip between it and the frame," said Boz. JJ and Boz searched the room from top to bottom. They couldn't find anything to use as a lever.

Boz sat on the floor in the middle of the room and rested his chin in his hands. "Perhaps we're going about this the wrong way," he suggested. "If we can't open the door, maybe we should leave by the window."

JJ opened the small metal-framed window and looked down to the rocks below. They seemed a long way off and made him feel dizzy. "We'd need a very long rope to reach the ground from here" he sighed.

He slammed the window shut and joined Boz on the floor. They would just have to wait for Guppy, or whoever the lighthouse keeper was, to return from wherever he was . . .

They both spotted the chest at about the same time. A corner of it was sticking out from under the metal-framed bed. The two boys leaped to their feet and dragged it out into the open. It looked like an old seaman's chest from a swashbuckling pirate story.

"There may be some rope in here," said JJ doubtfully. The lid wouldn't open. The hefty chest was locked.

16

Boz had spied a set of keys hanging on a hook by the stove, and hurried over to fetch them. After a few false starts, they found a key that fitted both of the locks perfectly. It was obvious that the old chest hadn't been opened for years. The locks creaked and squeaked in protest as the key released the rusty mechanisms.

Throwing back the lid, Boz and JJ were rewarded with the intriguing sight of ancient charts, old books, a ship-in-a-bottle, and curious hodge podge of items to do with sailing and the sea.

All thoughts of escaping were forgotten as the two brothers began studying the contents of the trunk. Boz picked up an old leather bound book and began to read. What he read was so vivid, so gripping, that it somehow came alive for him. He could almost see the events unfolding like a play . . .

17

A Tale of Treachery

This is incredible. Listen.

. . . The year is 1783. The place is Dungeon Creek.

At night, its treacherous rocks are lighted with lanterns to warn passing ships to steer clear.

I feel a storm brewing.

But a gang of local villains who call themselves 'wreckers' have other ideas. They snuff out the lanterns on the rocks . . .

. . . and light one of their own on the beach to trick the ships into coming too close inland . . .

Ooh, there'll be rich pickings tonight.

. . . so that they smash on to the rocks.

CRUNCH!

As a ship begins to sink, the wreckers leap on board and steal the cargo by force . . .

6

. . . ignoring the desperate pleas of trapped or drowning sailors.

Help me! Please help me.

7

There are many wrecker gangs along the coastline . . .

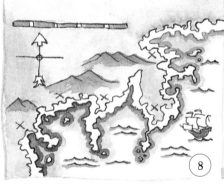

8

. . . but few are as successful and feared as the wreckers of Dungeon Creek.

Here's to the next dark night.

And to foolish captains.

9

It is only a matter of time before a high price is put on their heads.

WANTED
DEAD or Aliv
he most dr
crimes of sh
ecking, murde
and plundering.
he name of th
u are here
ded t

10

To think that all happened here just over two hundred years ago.

Escape and Failure

It was beginning to get dark as Boz and JJ sat in the circular room thinking about the evil wreckers of years gone by.

Now that there was a proper lighthouse in Dungeon Creek, there was no fear of any modern ships striking the rocks below.

Their thoughts were interrupted by a loud hum of electricity as the huge revolving light came to life in the lamp room above them. They looked up in amazement, startled by the noise.

"This lighthouse must be on an automatic time switch," said Boz.

"That means that there's no need to have a lighthouse keeper any more," sighed JJ. "I don't think anyone has slept in that bed for a very long time."

A mouse stared out at them from a hole in the mattress.

"*We* may have to sleep in it," Boz pointed out. "It could be days or even months before anyone finds us."

All this talk of beds gave Boz a flash of inspiration. He went over to the huge wardrobe that he had searched earlier, and took some faded sheets from inside one of the drawers.

"I don't know why I didn't think of this before!" he said excitedly. "I've had one of my great ideas." JJ looked more than a little doubtful.

The 'great idea' was to tie the sheets together to make a rope. It wasn't nearly long enough to reach all the way down to the ground. However, it was long enough for them to climb out of the window and in through the one below.

JJ went first. The brothers had tossed a coin to see who it would be, and JJ had lost. The vicious wind lashed against him as he clung to the rope. Once he almost lost his glasses, then his grip as he pushed them back up his nose. One slip and he could end up falling onto the rocks below.

He made it! Pushing the lower window open with his feet, he found himself back in the spiral stairwell. Boz soon followed him.

They hurried down the stairs and threw open the front door, only to find that the tide had risen. The rock path they'd crossed from the beach was now covered by crashing waves. They were trapped for the night after all.

Rescue from the Rocks

Out of the darkness a small boat appeared, rowed through the foaming waves by a girl with chestnut brown hair. With great skill, she brought the tiny wooden craft as close to Boz and JJ as she could. Just below the surface of the sea lurked the dangerous rocks that could rip the boat to shreds.

"Step into the water there," the girl pointed. "It's shallow, but be careful not to slip," she cried above the wind.

JJ and Boz did as she commanded, wading over to the boat and clambering into it. Immediately, the girl began rowing away into deeper, safer water. Every time the sweeping path of light from the revolving lighthouse lamp illuminated the boat, its three occupants took on an eerie glow.

"Thank you for saving us," said Boz. "JJ and I didn't fancy spending a cold night in a lighthouse." A seagull screeched with laughter somewhere in the sky. "You haven't told us your name."

"Katherine," she said, her eyes glinting in the twilight. "My name is Katherine. You must be careful of Dungeon Creek's treacherous tides."

It only took a few minutes for the boat to reach the shore. It was then that Boz and JJ were in for yet another surprise. When Katherine had beached the boat in a particular place on the sand, she used her arms to swing herself out of the boat and into an enormous old-fashioned wheelchair.

Katherine was aware of Boz and JJ's amazement. "What's the big deal?" she asked. "You're pretty acrobatic yourselves, swinging through the lighthouse window like that. It was the white sheets that caught my eye."

"It was lucky you spotted us," said JJ. They followed Katherine up a ramp designed for boats to slide down to the water, and found themselves on a flat path running between the cliffs.

Katherine asked what they'd been doing in the lighthouse. "Trying to find out more about a man named Silas Guppy," JJ told her with caution.

"There's been a Silas Guppy in Dungeon Creek for hundreds of years," said Katherine. "And the last six of them have all been lighthouse keepers."

"You mean there's more than one Silas Guppy?" asked Boz, feeling very foolish. Why hadn't he thought of such an obvious explanation?

A smile passed across Katherine's lips. "Of course," she said. "Every first son of a Silas Guppy was called Silas all the way down through the years. The very last Silas Guppy was the very last lighthouse keeper. He never had a son so, when he died, it was decided to control the lighthouse with electric machinery."

"Were all the Silas Guppys painters too?" asked JJ.

"Painters? I was wondering if that was why you went to the lighthouse," said Katherine, bringing her wheelchair to a halt. "I believe you have something of mine and I want it back." A strange expression crossed Katherine's face. For that one fleeting moment, she reminded Boz of another face – one that was beginning to haunt him. It was a face created from brushstrokes and oil paint by a man named Guppy. Katherine had looked exactly like the woman in the painting.

A Name at Last

Boz, JJ and Katherine made their way to Mr. Barkis's cottage in silence. Katherine hadn't been invited, but there was an unspoken understanding that she should go back with them. After all, she had rescued them hadn't she? And she knew about their painting, even claiming that it was hers.

Mr. Barkis didn't seem at all surprised or worried that they'd returned from a 'trip to the library' so late and so wet. They found him in his workshop. It was the first time the boys had been right inside. Their host was busy whipping a table using strips of rope studded with small nails.

"This makes a piece of wood look old," he quickly explained. "It's called distressing it. I'm doing two or three hundred years' worth of damage to this table in one evening. By the time I've finished with it, it will look like a genuine antique."

JJ introduced Katherine to Mr. Barkis. "Oh, I know Katherine and she knows me," he said. "How's your Aunt Lilian, Katherine?"

"As gloomy as ever," grinned Katherine. "I'm here about the oil painting, Mr. Barkis. My aunt had no right to sell it to JJ and Boz. It belongs to me."

"Oh, it's *that* painting is it? Well, that's for your aunt and you three to sort out between you," said Barkis. "Why not go inside and talk it over?"

Mr. Barkis makes copies of antique furniture.

When Katherine entered the cottage, she caught sight of the painting. The flickering glow of an old oil lamp cast a strange glow on the canvas. The painted waves appeared to be moving like the real thing. "You've cleaned it!" she cried. "You've uncovered *her*." Then Katherine spotted the Latin inscription. "What's this?" she asked, moving closer.

For reasons he couldn't explain, Boz was reluctant to tell Katherine anything just yet. Perhaps it was because he felt that she was hiding things from them.

"The ship in the background is supposed to be the very last ship smashed on the rocks in Dungeon Creek by the wreckers," she told them, with a shudder.

"Have you any idea who the woman in the painting is?" asked Boz. Katherine had obviously known about her, even though her image had been covered in centuries of grime.

"Oh yes," replied Katherine, her eyes avoiding theirs. "I know about *her*. Her name was Reckless Rose. She was leader of the Dungeon Creek wreckers." It was she who lured so many ships to the trecherous rock and so many unsuspecting sailors to their doom."

At last they knew the name of the woman whose face had been crowding Boz's mind since he first laid eyes on the painting "She was supposed to be a witch," said Katheine quietly. Boz and JJ looked at each other.

"Superstitious old garbage," said JJ, watching the waves on the canvas with a queasy feeling inside.

"That's as maybe," said Katherine. "But I am a direct descendant of Rose, and some people take that garbage very seriously indeed."

Katherine's Tale

For JJ it was simply exciting to learn more about the painting, and to meet someone related to a so-called witch. To Boz, Katherine's news was much more than that. Somehow Reckless Rose had been haunting his thoughts ever since the moment the painting had been cleaned. Now he knew her name.

"What happened to Reckless Rose?" asked JJ. He had heard about the treatment of so-called witches in history lessons.

"Now there's a story," said Katherine, and she began her strange tale, filling their minds with images of past deeds . . .

After years of rich picking from helpless drowning sailors . . .

. . . Rose and her wreckers were finally caught by the army of 'Redcoats'.

She wasn't put on trial with the rest of her gang . . .

. . . but was declared to be a witch. Yes, the God-fearing people of Dungeon Creek still believed in witches.

Rose was dragged from her prison cell to be burned at the stake . . .

. . . But legend has it that the fire couldn't harm her. She stepped through the flames and walked away.

"What happened next?" asked JJ when Katherine had finished her story. If Rose had survived the fire, then maybe she really did have strange powers.

Katherine shrugged. "No one knows. She simply disappeared. She left behind a daughter, called Sara. Sara was brought up by the Silas Guppy of the time. He treated her as his own child and painted a picture of Rose for Sara to remember her mother by. When Sara grew up, she married and had a daughter, and passed on the painting to her."

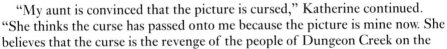

"And she handed it on to *her* daughter, and so on, right down the years until *you* inherited it?" said Boz. "Amazing."

He and JJ stared into the painting, wondering what became of Reckless Rose herself. This was no ordinary picture. He had no doubt about that.

"My aunt is convinced that the picture is cursed," Katherine continued. "She thinks the curse has passed onto me because the picture is mine now. She believes that the curse is the revenge of the people of Dungeon Creek on the family of the woman who lured sailors to their doom . . . or so she says."

The room fell silent and Boz and JJ turned to stare into the fire. Watching the yellow and orange flames licking the small pile of logs, they thought back to the horrors of the days when people could be burned as witches and of the horrors of Rose's crimes.

Then Boz's thoughts returned to the painting with its strange Latin inscription. "Hang on," he gulped. "If the painting itself is cursed, and we now own it, that can only mean one thing. The curse has been passed on to us. *We're* cursed!"

The Stranger

"Nonsense!" said Mr. Barkis, his moonlit figure framed in the open doorway. "It's time that you went home Katherine. I'll drive you. Now, you two had better make yourself something to eat then go up to bed."

When Mr. Barkis got back from the house where Katherine lived with her Aunt Lilian, Boz and JJ were finishing their supper. "Don't start filling your heads with ideas about witches and curses," he said. "Katherine's aunt has a great deal to answer for. She thinks Katherine is in a wheelchair because of that stupid curse."

"That's ridiculous," said JJ in disbelief. "There are plenty of people in wheelchairs."

"You should see Katherine rowing a boat," said Boz. "She could beat me in a race anyday."

"Exactly," said Mr. Barkis. "Lilian Smallweed has some very outdated ideas. If I'd known this was the Reckless Rose picture, I'd have burned it the minute you brought it through that door . . ." His eyes lit up. "In fact, I think that's what I'll do right now."

Barkis snatched the oil painting and marched over to the fire. "No! Wait!" cried JJ. "Don't do that, Mr. Barkis. Surely it's for Katherine to decide what to do with the . . ."

But he was too late, or he would have been if something very strange hadn't happened. Before the painting reached the fireplace, a window crashed open and an incredible gust of wind blew into the room.

Papers were blown off a desk. A vase fell to the floor and shattered. And the flames of the fire were blown out in an instant.

The painting landed with a THUD in the harmless pile of ashes. JJ and Boz shuddered. For the first time since they'd arrived in Dungeon Creek, Mr. Barkis actually seemed slightly bothered. "Maybe it isn't right for me to destroy the painting," he mumbled. "Now, off to bed you two."

The next morning, Boz and JJ decided to return the painting to Katherine. Barkis told them the way to her house, and off they went. They took turns in carrying the painting because it had become strangely heavy.

As they were walking toward the village, a sleek black limousine pulled up alongside them. Even the windows were black, so they couldn't see inside. A very tall man stepped out of the car. He had strange eyes and a small pointed beard on the tip of his chin. His hair was silver. He reminded Boz of a goat.

The stranger blocked their path. He towered above them, staring over their heads into the distance. "You will give me the painting," he stated. His voice was strangely hypnotic. "NOW, " he added, as his eyes met theirs. They seemed to burn like red hot coals, and the boys began to feel scared.

Before Boz even had time to think, the man shot his arms out with lightning speed and snatched the painting from his grasp. He held their gaze for one moment longer, then leaped back into his car, barking an order to his driver. The limousine sped off at extremely high speed, leaving Boz and JJ trembling, with the stranger's gleeful laughter ringing in their ears.

A Confession and Confrontation

Not knowing what to do, JJ and Boz hurried to the house where Katherine lived with her Aunt Lilian. Once inside, they told Katherine and her aunt what had happened. Katherine was horrified by the description of the man.

"How terrible," she said. "He's doesn't sound like anyone I know from around here – more like some spook in a horror movie."

"A stranger in Dungeon Creek," said Aunt Lilian mysteriously. "What would he be wanting with my Katherine's painting?"

"I thought you'd just be glad it's gone," said JJ. "After all, you did sell it to us to pass on the curse."

The woman blushed. "No, my dears. That's not quite right. I believe that the curse only falls on direct descendants of Reckless Rose. I thought that if I could sell it to someone outside the family who was willing to buy it, the curse would be broken. You haven't bought the curse, just a harmless old painting."

You boys have nothing to fear from the painting.

"What I want to know is how we can find the painting and get it back," said Boz . "Curse or no curse, Mrs. Smallweed, that is no ordinary painting. I'm sure . . . I'm sure that Reckless Rose is somehow trying to speak to me through it!" There was a stunned silence, only broken by a cry from JJ.

"Of course!" he cried. "It must have been goat-features who tried to steal the painting from the cottage the other night."

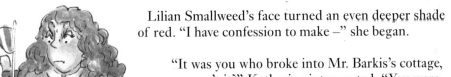

Lilian Smallweed's face turned an even deeper shade of red. "I have confession to make –" she began.

"It was you who broke into Mr. Barkis's cottage, wasn't it?" Katherine interrupted. "You were trying to steal the painting back. But why? I thought you'd be delighted to have it out of this house at last."

"I thought JJ and Boz were just passing through," she explained. "When I discovered that they were staying in Dungeon Creek, I realized that the painting would be too. I did it for *you*, Katherine."

Katherine spun her wheelchair around and headed down the hall for the front door. "You did it for me? You're crazy, Aunt Lilian. You're the one who believes in the curse, not me. Listen to yourself. You're not making any sense," she shouted. "One minute you say I'm 'saved' if the painting's sold. The next minute you say it has to leave the village! You don't know what to believe."

At that moment, without warning, the front door was thrown wide open.

Dazzling sunlight poured into the hallway. The brightness almost blinded them. Boz and JJ put their hands up to their faces to shield their eyes. "This is not what I want," said a familiar hypnotic voice. "You have tried to deceive me, children. What a very sad and foolish thing to do."

Something was thrown through the air and landed at Katherine's feet with a crash. It was the painting of Reckless Rose.

Unspoken Threats

As Boz and JJ's eyes became more used to the sunlight, they could make out the form of the frightening stranger. Though his voice was calm, his face was filled with rage. He didn't remind JJ of a goat anymore. He reminded him of a picture of a devil he'd seen somewhere. A picture that had given him terrifying nightmares.

"Oh, children," said the man. "Did you really think that you could trick me with this painting? In the original, the ship is much farther out to sea! This is a copy. A good copy, I'll grant you, but a fake."

Lilian Smallweed's jaw dropped wide open. She stared at the intruder but didn't do anything except mutter. She looked like an animal frozen with fear by the headlights of an oncoming car.

I know who you are . . . I know you . . .

Katherine looked down at the painting. The man was right. The ship did look closer than before. "You can't fool me," she said. "You still have the original yourself. How dare you steal my painting then show up here with a fake. What's your game?" If she felt threatened by the man, it didn't show.

The stranger stormed over to the painting and snatched it up. "Don't lie to me, witch child. This is the picture the boys gave me. Look at the frame. Look at the back of the canvas," he snarled.

Is it the original?

The three children studied the picture. Everything about it was identical to the original, except that the ship was painted bigger so it looked nearer Reckless Rose and the shoreline.

Katherine glanced over to her aunt. Why wasn't she ordering this man out of their home? She simply sat there muttering: "You're Krowley. You're Doctor Krowley. I know your face . . . I know . . . "

JJ felt it was time to act. "If you don't leave right this second, I'll call the police. You're a thief and a bully," he said.

The stranger laughed his horrible laugh. "The police? Oh, foolish child. There are forces at work here that no police force in the world can stop! The old woman recognizes me, and speaks no words of disrespect. You should take a lesson from her. I shall be back, and I want the original painting. Clear?"

He didn't wait for an answer, but turned and walked out of the house, down the path and into his waiting black limousine.

"But this *is* the original painting," said Boz in amazement. He touched the figure of Reckless Rose. "I can sense it . . . I know it. Somehow, the ship really has moved. It looks bigger because it is getting closer to the rocks. In its own way, the picture is alive . . . " Behind him, Katherine's aunt let out a long and dreadful wail.

Back to the Lighthouse

They asked if anyone around the village had seen a goat-like stranger, or a black car, or knew anything about the name 'Doctor Krowley'. They drew a blank.

Ain't seen anyone like that 'round 'ere.

"He can't have vanished into thin air," said JJ.

"Why not?" said Boz glumly. "He looked a bit like a magician to me."

"He *is* very creepy," said his brother. "He wants the original painting and doesn't believe this is it. So what are we going to tell him when he comes back? He doesn't seem the type of man who would listen to reason."

"What worries me is that sooner or later, the man my aunt calls Krowley is going to discover his mistake. He'll realize that this *is* the original painting and that some strange force is making it change. Either way, we're in trouble," said Katherine, resting her chin in her hands.

They headed back to Mr. Barkis's cottage in silence for a while. Katherine had left Aunt Lilian tucked up in bed. The morning's events had seemed too much for her, but she'd refused any suggestions of calling a doctor.

"We're going to have to hide the painting," said JJ at last. "Somewhere that Krowley will never think of looking."

"I know the perfect place," said Katherine, her face breaking into a grin.

That night, Katherine rowed the two boys the short distance to the lighthouse. Boz and JJ jumped out of the boat and pulled it onto a smooth flat rock. They helped Katherine out of the boat to the front step of the lighthouse, where she sat down.

JJ went back to the boat and pulled out the painting, which Mr. Barkis had wrapped in an old blanket. Katherine's idea of bringing the painting here to hide it under cover of darkness seemed a good one.

Leaving Katherine to keep watch, Boz and JJ made their way up the stairs. They found the door to the circular room open. JJ leaned a chair against it to stop it blowing shut. "I wouldn't fancy having to swing through the downstairs window a second time," he said.

The sheets were still tied in position where they'd left them. They hauled them back in through the window. They didn't want anything odd catching Doctor Krowley's eye and attracting him to the lighthouse.

Before sliding it under the bed, they took one last look at the painting that was causing them so much trouble. The ship looked even bigger now. Yes, even closer to the treacherous rocks.

They hurried back down the stairs to Katherine, at least to where she should have been. She was nowhere in sight.

The boat was missing too. What was happening? Where had she gone, leaving them all alone?

"Where's Rose? Where's Rose?" screeched the myna bird, circling above them in the night sky.

Danger in the Dark

Boz shook his head in dismay. "It was a trick!" he moaned. "Katherine's left us stranded. I knew we should never have trusted her."

"Don't be so stupid," said JJ. "You're as bad as her aunt. What would be the point of leaving us here? When the tide goes out, we can walk back across the string of rocks."

"Then something must have happened to her," said Boz. They peered into the blackness of the night, following the sweeping beam of the lighthouse's huge lamp.

Less than a mile away, out to sea, Captain Weller of the cargo ship *Dickens* stepped into the wheelhouse of his ship and took over the helm. He turned the *Dickens* twenty degrees starboard. "We should be able to see the lighthouse soon," he said.

Meanwhile, Boz and JJ's hunt for Katherine was fruitless "I hope she's all right . . ." began JJ. At that moment there was a loud FIZZ and everything went pitch black. The huge revolving lamp at the top of the lighthouse had gone out.

"Great," sighed Boz. "That's all we need. That painting has even put a jinx on the lighthouse now."

Back on the *Dickens*, Captain Weller frowned. He was sure he had seen a flash of light, but now it was gone. It must have been lightning. He glanced down at his navigation chart. They would be reaching the dangerous coastline of Dungeon Creek soon. Thank heavens for the lighthouse to guide them.

At that same moment, on the rocks, JJ had a terrible thought. The lighthouse was there for a very special reason. It was there to warn ships away from the rocks. The danger was as great today as it had been in the time of the wreckers.

"Boz!" he cried, finding his brother's arm and grabbing it in the dark. "Can't you see what's happening? Reckless Rose is doing more than trying to speak to you through the painting. That witch is trying to reach out through the centuries to cause her first shipwreck in two hundred years! Maybe she's even using us to do it. We brought the painting here."

"But there aren't any ships around," began Boz. His words were drowned out by the deep and deafening sound of a ship's horn.

Unaware of the danger that lay ahead in the darkness, Captain Weller turned the helm of the *Dickens* and headed straight for the rocks of Dungeon Creek. The very rocks upon which Reckless Rose had stood two hundred years before.

Disaster on the Waves

Boz and JJ hurried up the winding dark staircase to the round room. Fumbling in the dark, they found the candles and matches that they remembered having seen in the trunk.

JJ tried striking several matches before one flared to life with a spluttering flame. The damp sea air hadn't helped, neither had his shaking hands.

They quickly lighted the candles, the faces of the many Silas Guppys stared from the wall, watching them in the eerie glow.

Now JJ and Boz had a far harder task. They had to try to get the huge light to work to warn the ship away from the rocks. Each holding a candle, they climbed the ladder to the lamp room.

In the middle of lamp room was what looked like an enormous electric globe, and a mechanism which was supposed to swivel around it to create the 'flashing' of the light. The mechanism was still, and the globe dead.

The villagers will have seen the light go out.

But they'll be too late to stop this ship hitting the rocks.

Around the outside of the room was a metal walkway, and huge glass windows overlooking both the land and sea.

JJ and Boz peered out into the night to see if they could spot the ship they'd heard. They dashed from one side to the other, straining their eyes in a frantic bid to find the vessel.

"There it is!" cried Boz, at last. He pointed to the *Dickens* moving toward them in the inky gloom. "Couldn't we light a fire in here to warn them?"

"By the time the flames are big enough for anyone to see, the ship will have been ripped to shreds on the rocks!" cried JJ. "And we brought the picture and its curse here. It's all our fault!"

In True Need

Boz and JJ hurried back down to the round room. "We only have one chance left," said Boz. "Our shouts will never be heard, and we can't get back to the village to get help. We'll have to try the painting."

"What? What do you mean?" asked JJ. "It's the painting that got us into this mess. Katherine's Aunt Lilian was right all along. It's cursed. It's evil."

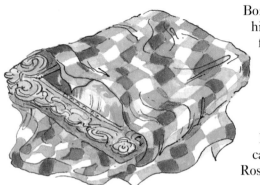

Boz pulled the painting out from its hiding place under the bed. It lay on the floor in front of them, still covered in a blanket. "Do you remember what the inscription said? '*If you truly need me, say my name and I shall be there to aid you.*' Don't you see, JJ? If we call out Reckless Rose's name, and really need her help, she will come to our aid. We can call her up. We can *summon* Reckless Rose to save the ship."

"Have you gone mad, Boz? It's a trick. It must be. Reckless Rose is probably causing all this trouble just so that you'll summon her up and let her loose on the world again," JJ argued. "If she can do all this when she's in a painting, think what she might be able to do if you call her up!"

"But she may have to do as we say if we summon her," said Boz. "Like a genie in a bottle . . . I don't know. We've got to try something, JJ."

Time was running out. The *Dickens* was drawing closer and closer to the rocks. Without the light of the Dungeon Creek lighthouse to guide it, Captain Weller and his crew had no idea that they were so far inland, so close to the jagged rocks, and so near disaster.

JJ pulled the blanket off the painting. In the strange glow of candlelight, the ship seemed enormous now, as though it was right by the rocks. Reckless Rose looked just the same as she always had . . . or was the expression on her face a little more triumphant?

"Right," said Boz, leaping to his feet. "I'm going to summon Rose now." As if on cue, the fog horn of the *Dickens* sounded once again – much louder and nearer this time. The brothers trembled, and the wind lashed against the tiny window, rattling it in its frame.

Outside, the waves began to pound against the base of Dungeon Creek lighthouse, and seaspray battered against the glass of the lamp room. JJ was about to protest again, then caved in. "Maybe we can save that ship and its crew out there . . . or maybe all this is mumbo jumbo, so it won't make any difference anyway."

Just then, something caught JJ's eye. Something in the picture seemed to glint. He peered at it more closely. It was a row of tiny letters on the side of the ship. "Look. I've never seen these before!" he said.

"That's because the ship has never been close enough before. I told you that it was alive, didn't I?"cried Boz.

In amazement, the brothers read the name of the ship in the painting out loud. "The *Empress*!"

Moments later, there was a terrifying noise. It filled the air, and Dungeon Creek lighthouse shook to its very foundations.

From the Watery Grave

Boz and JJ rushed up to the lamp room. They wanted to see if the awful noise was the rocks ripping apart the hull of the cargo ship.

Below, a strange gust of wind blew a candle onto the floor. Its flame began to lick and burn the edge of an old navigation chart. Through the huge glass windows, they looked down at the scene out to sea. What they saw left them speechless.

The *Dickens* hadn't hit the rocks. It was still heading straight for them . . . What was making such an unnerving sound, filling the air around them? Between the ship and the rocks, there was a strange patch of water. . . glimmering . . . glowing. It was almost as if the moon itself was trapped beneath the waves, sending out its silvery light.

The shimmering water began to bubble like a witch's cauldron. Suddenly, an eerie ship with tattered sails broke through the surface of the waves with a resounding crash. Its ancient rigging creaked in the howling wind. Everywhere was bathed in a glowing silver light.

"'*If you truly need me, say my name and I shall be there to aid you*'," JJ yelled above the noise. "It wasn't Reckless Rose we could call out to for help. It was the ship in the painting. It was the *Empress*!"

On the bridge of the *Dickens*, the stunned captain couldn't believe his eyes. With a spin of the helm, he quickly changed course to avoid the eerie sight, and steered his rusting vessel away from the danger of the hidden rocks of Dungeon Creek.

Scuppered Plans

From their vantage point up in the lamp room, Boz and JJ stood, open mouthed, watching the miraculous events unfold below them. The night sky was illuminated by the silvery glow of the *Empress*. Then, and only then, did they spot something else. A small speedboat, bobbing anchored in the water. Someone else had witnessed these extraordinary events.

Katherine's tiny boat was attached to the speedboat by a rope. In the front of the speedboat stood Dr. Krowley. He was staring at the shimmering *Empress*, a mad glint in his eyes.

"He must have followed us here and kidnapped Katherine when we went upstairs," groaned Boz. "He'll probably keep her prisoner until we give him the painting. He certainly knows something about its power . . . and will obviously stop at nothing until he gets it. That man is pure evil."

Dr. Krowley turned his head and stared straight up at the top of the lighthouse where the brothers were still standing. Although they couldn't even see his eyes from that distance, they somehow felt his penetrating gaze. He threw his head back like a wolf howling at the moon and began to shout into the night.

JJ and Boz hurried onto a small balcony which ran around the outside of the lamp room, and caught Krowley's words in the wind. "I have the witch child, now I must have the power of the painting!" he wailed.

Some of Krowley's words were drowned out by the crashing waves, or were lost when the wind changed direction. In these moments, he seemed even more enraged, like some villain in a silent film with a fist raised in anger.

The words that came through loud and clear made Boz and JJ shudder. "I know that you are up there boys. Distance and darkness do not hinder my sight. You have something I want or who knows what might happen to your poor little friend here?"

JJ and Boz knew that they would have to let him have the painting. All that mattered was that Katherine should be released unharmed.

What Krowley didn't notice was that his prisoner, Katherine, was pulling herself forward. JJ and Boz watched as she lifted up one of the oars from her boat and swung it straight at him.

The edge of the oar hit the back of Krowley's knees. With the roar of an injured animal, he toppled headfirst into the silver sea. At that precise moment, there was a deafening BOOM, followed by a splintering of glass. Sparks began to fly around the lamp room.

A Few Days Later

"It's funny how newspapers always come up with such ordinary explanations for such extraordinary events," said JJ looking at the clippings Katherine was sticking in a scrapbook.

Washed up wreck saves ship from rocks

from our own correspondent

A 200-year-old ship rose from its watery grave in Dungeon Creek last Thursday night. This freak incident saved serious damage, and possible injury, to the *Dickens* and its crew. The *Dickens*, an Usbornian registered vessel, changed course to avoid the wreck, at the same time narrowly missing the notoriously dangerous rocks at Dungeon Creek.

According to experts, the *Empress* is in remarkably good condition. "It must have been preserved in thick mud on the sea bed," Alex Heep, a professor of marine archeology, told reporters.

Lighthouse destroyed in electrical fire

from our Dungeon Creek correspondent

Dungeon Creek lighthouse, a popular local landmark, has been badly damaged by fire. For generations, the lighthouse was looked after by the Guppy family. Each Guppy named 'Silas' inherited the job from the Silas Guppy before him. It was only when the last Silas Guppy died without a son, that the lighthouse became fully automatic. "It was an extremely hot fire, and did an extraordinary amount of damage," said the local fire chief.

EVIL 'WIZARD' KROWLEY CAPTURED
THANKS TO DESCENDANT OF RECKLESS ROSE

Thanks to the quick thinking of Ms. Lilian Smallweed and her niece Katherine, the notorious Dr. Kaleb Krowley was back behind bars last night. Dr. Krowley, who claims to be a Grand Wizard of the Order of Evil, is wanted in seven different countries in connection with about crimes from theft to kidnapping.

Ms. Smallweed, a local expert on the ancient customs of so-called witchcraft and magic, recognized Krowley from a photograph in a book of witchcraft she had read. "He sensed this, and put me in some kind of trance," she claims. "When I snapped out of it, I informed the police at once." But help was at hand from her own family. In events that have not yet been released to the newspapers, ... Katherine was one of a

Dr. Krowley

group of three people to take the dripping wet Dr. Krowley to the authorit... Katherine is a direct descendant of local folk legend Reckless Rose, was the leader of the Wreckers.

"And there's no mention of our brave efforts to warn that ship, or Katherine bringing the boat alongside the lighthouse when the fire broke out," said Boz. "But they've made your aunt out to be some kind of a hero." He laughed.

"I'm just happy it all ended well," said Katherine. "The painting wasn't a force for evil, but a force for good. Aunt Lilian was quite wrong."

The other two nodded. "The Silas Guppy who painted the picture and gave it to Rose's daughter was somehow trying to bring *good* luck to your family," said Boz. "Perhaps to give them a chance to do something right after all of Reckless Rose's wrong-doings."

"Warning the *Dickens* and clobbering Krowley was certainly the right thing to do," added JJ.

"I may be in a wheelchair, but I'm no pushover," said Katherine. "He's the one who was pushed over . . . over*board*." They all laughed. She closed the scrapbook.

"It's a shame that the painting was destroyed in the fire," said Boz. "I suppose once it had served its purpose . . ." He shrugged.

"The painting wasn't entirely destroyed," said Katherine. From under the scrapbook she produced the only remaining piece of the painting and passed it to Boz and JJ.

It was just a small piece of the canvas, with charred edges. On it was Reckless Rose. There wasn't so much as a speck of soot on her. She was entirely undamaged. Once again, the so-called witch of Dungeon Creek had escaped the flames.

Did You Spot?

You can use this page to help spot things that could be useful in solving the mystery. First, there are hints and clues you can read as you go along. They will give you some idea of what to look out for. Then there are extra notes to read which tell you more about what happened afterwards.

Hints and Clues

3　Look at the items on the stall carefully. You may come across some similar objects later on.

4-5　Try to familiarize yourself with the painting.

6-7　Remember what the intruder is wearing, and keep your eyes peeled.

8-9　Shadows can reveal a great deal about a person.

10-11　Familiar names and familiar figures.

12-13　Something in the grass might raise its ugly head in the not too distant future.

14-15　Think about Silas Guppy. There must be a simple solution.

16-17　It's worth remembering the things in the old chest. Something could come in handy later on.

18-19　Are there any familiar faces in this tale?

20-21　Look closely. Is help at hand?

22-23　Katherine probably knows more than she is prepared to say at present.

24-25　Mr. Barkis has a few familiar objects in his workshop. Look closely.

26-27　Wreckers and witches? This must be of some importance.

28-29　The stick that the goat-like stranger is carrying has appeared somewhere before.

34-35　The myna bird has something strange to say.

36-37　If Katherine hasn't gone off on her own, who might have taken her? And why?

40-41　Boz and JJ have said the name of the ship in the painting. That must be important.

42-43　Everything should be falling into place by now.

In the End

There was a reward for the capture of Dr. Krowley. Katherine spent some of the money buying a better wheelchair, designed for getting about faster.

The only remaining piece of the painting is now in a glass case in Dungeon Creek Museum.

Mr. Barkis was interviewed by local police about his fake antiques being sold as the real thing. It turned out that he knew nothing about it. He had sold them as copies to a man from the city.

When foundations were laid to build the new lighthouse, the builders found an old skeleton. Katherine thinks that they are the bones of Reckless Rose, found at last after two hundred years.

The myna bird, that JJ has now named 'Beakie', is a direct descendant of the myna bird owned by the Silas Guppy who painted Reckless Rose.

By the Way . . .

Did you spot:

It was Aunt Lilian casting the shadow on page 9.

Krowley dropped his stick outside the lighthouse before Boz and JJ visited it for the first time.

The jail Reckless Rose was held in was an old cave with bars set into the rock. This was the old dungeon which Dungeon Creek was named after.

First published in 1994 by Usborne Publishing Ltd, Usborne House, 83-85 Saffron Hill, London EC1N 8RT, England.

Copyright © 1994 Usborne Publishing Ltd
The name Usborne and the device 🎈 are Trade Marks of Usborne Publishing Ltd.